About the Author

Sonita Singh is an award winning screenwriter and film maker. From a young age, Sonita loved to read. She loved everything about it and would pour over books. Reading for hours on end, until her eyes were so sore she had to stop. Only to think about the story. About the words. She would become so enthralled in the story that she would become lost. Once again thinking about it for hours.

As a child, Sonita knew in her heart what her passion was… to write.

A multi-international award winning screenwriter and film maker, *Butterfly Kisses* is Sonita's first children's book.

sonita singh

BUTTERFLY
KISSES

AUSTIN MACAULEY PUBLISHERS™

LONDON • CAMBRIDGE • NEW YORK • SHARJAH

A CIP catalogue record for this title is available from the British Library.

ISBN 9781788237994 (Paperback)
ISBN 9781788238007 (Hardback)
ISBN 9781788238014 (E-Book)

www.austinmacauley.com

First Published (2018)
Austin Macauley Publishers™ Ltd.
25 Canada Square
Canary Wharf
London
E14 5LQ

Dedication

For my angels

Jaime, Amelia and Noah.

Love you now, forever and always.

I want to thank my beautiful children, your love and belief is my strength.

To Helen Ibrahim – you are the most talented artist. Thank you for giving my words life in these breathtaking illustrations.

To all those who have walked beside me, I thank you from my heart to yours.

last night, my daddy died.

i am not really sure what died means.

i just want my daddy to come home.

where is he?

my mummy is sad.

she is crying.

i don't want to cry because i know my
daddy is coming home to us.

he always comes home.
he is coming home.

isn't he?

everyone was telling me that god needed him in heaven.
what did god need him for?

i need him.

i want my daddy.

so i spoke to god.

"please god, can i have my daddy back now?"

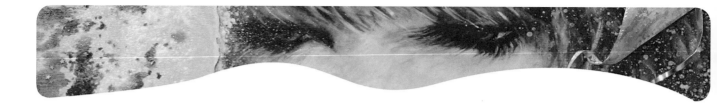

i waited and waited for my daddy to come back home.

but he didn't.

i know i will Play hide and seek.
daddy loved that game.

"daddy!
daddy!

come out, come out, wherever you are."

i searched and searched in all his favourite hiding spots.

"**daddy!**
daddy!

where are you?

i'll come find you.
you can't hide from me."

but i couldn't find him.
i will just keep looking and looking.

i won't stop!

Please god send my daddy home now.

god

didn't send my daddy home.

my mummy told me that daddy went to heaven.

where is heaven?

i will just go there and get my daddy.
mummy told me that heaven is all around us.
how can i get to everywhere?

how will i bring him home?

mummy told me that to see people in heaven,

we need to feel them with our hearts.

mummy told me that my daddy's heart and
my heart are one and he is always with me in my heart.

i still want him to come back to me and mummy.

enough of this dying stuff.

i cried for my daddy.

i want him to swoosh me in his arms and kiss my tears away.
who will make my sadness go away?
who will tickle me and make me giggle?

who will love me like my daddy?

i just want my daddy.

i had an awesome dream last night.

my daddy and i were playing on the swings in the backyard.
he was back with me.

we were laughing and smiling.
my daddy swooshed me up in his arms and cuddled me.
he took all my sadness away.
he said that kisses from the butterflies are from him.

guess what!

a white butterfly flew to my cheek and kissed me.
i am not joking, really kissed me.

my daddy kissed me from heaven.

i could feel my daddy in my heart.
i was sad i could not see him.
but i know that he is always with me.

i miss you daddy.

i love you.

and the white butterfly kissed me again.